Sherlock Holmes

and the

Final Reveal

By

Chris Gay

Gay, Chris
Suesea Press
Manchester, Connecticut
The Passion of the Chris, LLC

Cover design by Debbie Tosun Kilday
Interior Layout by Ryan Twomey-Allaire
Certain original characters created by Sir Arthur
Conan Doyle

ISBN 978-0-9844673-1-0

www.chrisjgay.com

Also by Chris Gay

Novels

Ghost of a Chance

Humor

And That's the Way It Was...Give or Take: A Daily Dose of My Radio Writings

Shouldn't Ice Cold Beer Be Frozen? My 365 Random Thoughts to Improve Your Life Not One Iota

The Bachelor Cookbook: Edible Meals with a Side of Sarcasm

Upcoming Humor Books

Another Round of Ice Cold Beer: My 365 More Random Thoughts to Improve Your Life Not One Iota

Something Witty this Way Comes

Upcoming Fiction

Perdition's Wrath

Dedication

For my great-aunt Genevieve; a truly remarkable person. There are few things I'm more proud of than to be able to call myself her great-nephew. Thank you, Aunt Gene, for always believing in me.

"There is nothing more deceptive than an obvious fact."

"You have probably never heard of Professor Moriarty."

–Sir Arthur Conan Doyle

Author's Note

A short time ago I was given an extraordinary set of recordings to transcribe by a courier who stipulated that, in exchange, I must maintain his anonymity. After agreeing to the condition, I was commissioned to set down the spoken words in book form and then publish them under my own name. To this I also agreed. We then listened to the audio (it had been transferred neatly onto a compact disc made from the antique tapes out of which it was recorded) so that the courier could be certain I fully understood the gravity of the content. When the disc had run its course I could barely believe my own ears, and asked him why I specifically was chosen for the task.

I was informed that he represented the wealthy British gentleman who possessed the original recordings, and to whom it was of the utmost importance that a foreign, overseas writer be utilized; if at all possible an American. That was the only explanation I received as to how I was selected for the assignment. After some consideration I thought it best not to ask any further questions, and so now that brings me to the matter at hand.

The words you are about to read were spoken well over seven decades ago by none other than Dr. John H. Watson, M.D., friend and confidant to the world's greatest detective, Sherlock Holmes. With them, Dr. Watson explains that the decision as to whether the tale contained within his recordings should ever be published would be left entirely to fate. Clearly fate has at last opted to intervene, and has made its choice.

Not to belabor or overstate the point, but the story which lies ahead is simply astonishing. I'm not certain that I would have believed it had the words not come directly from Dr.

Watson himself. I now invite you to decide for yourself whether or not you believe.

Christopher J. Gay
April 13th, 2013
Hartford, Connecticut USA

Foreword

In the years since the demise of my cherished friend, it has been frequently inquired of me just how many of our great adventures remain un-catalogued. While there was a long period in which I might confidently offer an accurate rejoinder, the present truth is that as more time passes even my best efforts can provide merely an estimate. Still, at this late stage I seem to find myself with more occasions to reflect on the rather diminutive selection of our stories that, for one reason or another, I had failed to chronicle. In point of fact, to be precise, one tale in particular.

As I now embark on my ninth decade of shuffling across this mortal coil, I have little doubt that the time is nearly upon when I shall once again have the opportunity to reminisce with my old companion in person. Time and its inexorable connection to mortality is a reality from which no man escapes. That truth being what it is I feel the moment has now arrived to set the record straight.

You'll forgive me if I appear hesitant to continue, as I'm quite certain that this will prove the concluding narrative to cap off what has been called of late, somewhat to my amusement, the Sherlock Holmes "Canon." (A generously over-descriptive noun which elevates my writing skills to an undeserved level) As such, I may linger somewhat in relaying the facts of this case, just as I might had I the foreknowledge that on a given day I would be viewing my last sunset.

As arthritis has stolen nearly all of my power

to write, I'll instead take this opportunity to use my Dictaphone to document what I am about to relate. This wondrous machine was a gift to Holmes, later bequeathed to me, in appreciation for his solving a case for the American inventor Alexander Graham Bell. That case in itself was worthy of the telling, and surely would have been if not for Holmes's promise to Mr. Bell to forever maintain its secrecy. In that spirit, I too shall carry it to my grave.

Moreover, I will be so bold as to state that the following account will certainly prove to be the more memorable tale; in fact it's likely to top them all. If you are wondering why it hasn't been previously disclosed, the reason will become self-evident as the story unfolds. If not, it surely will by its conclusion.

As I have no desire to see the publication of this communication prior to my own end, once completed these tapes will be carefully concealed within my current residence in London. I shall leave it to fate that they should be discovered by some future owner and transcribed for public consumption. In the event they someday are, I should like to state for the ages that I have never known a more talented man; a greater champion of good, than my friend Sherlock Holmes. If only I could have measured up to his standards, I should have been much the better for it.

Dr. John H. Watson, M.D.

30 June 1940

It was a seasonably warm day, which was to be expected as the calendar page had recently turned to July. I had only just entered my study and sat down when my housekeeper knocked upon the door.

"Come in, Sara," said I.

"There's a telegram for you, Doctor."

I glanced around while simultaneously patting the breast pocket of my shirt, and realized I'd left my reading glasses in my bed chamber. Sara, having been witness to this same act of forgetfulness on my part for some time now, right away understood its meaning.

"Shall I retrieve your glasses for you, sir?"

"No, thank you. Please read the missive aloud and save us both some inconvenience. I apologize for having grown old and absent-minded in your care, Sara. The steady erosion of one's faculties is indeed a nuisance."

Having heard on many prior occasions my complaints on the matter; she offered a silent smile in acknowledgement as she unfolded the telegram.

"It is dated 3 July, Doctor."

"Yes. Please do go on."

Sara cleared her throat and proceeded. "Watson. My end draws near. If no bother I should like to say good-bye to my dearest friend. If you're agreeable, please call on me soon. Holmes." Sara read the last part with a slight tremor in her voice. She then walked over to my desk and laid the paper down upon it.

"There, there now," I offered in an attempt to comfort her; but my heart wasn't in the effort.

"My sincerest condolences, sir. When will you be leaving?"

"At once." I picked up a train schedule from the

corner of my desk and looked it over. "There's a 3:30 to Sussex; that's the one. I'll go pack."

"How long will you be gone?" She asked in that same slightly quivering voice.

"As long as it takes, my dear. As long as it takes."

*   *   *

A motor-carriage taxi brought me to the station, at which point I boarded the 3:30 train for Sussex Downs. Once situated in my compartment I was finally alone with my thoughts. I am set to turn seventy-eight next week, and yet it seemed no more than a fortnight since Holmes and I had spent our first night together as flat mates in Baker Street. But as the saying goes, time and tide wait for no man. And as the wheels on the track drew me closer to my friend and his last dance with life before facing the inevitability we all must, I found myself in a state of reflection.

There were so many cases; so many adventures. Though I could not have known or at least appreciated it then, I realized now that I was indeed a lucky man; and in more ways than one. Having access to such a titanic intellect for so long was a blessing. Still, there was one thing on which I pondered greatly. A still-unsettled case that Holmes never fully solved, though on that fact I am quite certain he remains completely oblivious. The question became should I bother him with it, or let him go to his reward believing his perfect record remained intact? (While he has always considered the Irene Adler case a loss,

I do not. And as Holmes's de facto biographer, what I say literally goes.)

As the scenery rolled by I thought further on this; even moreso as the train reached the Sussex station. I hired another motor-carriage taxi to take me the rest of the way to the farm and it was there, on the final leg of my journey, that I decided Holmes should know. Moreover, that he deserved to know. At several times throughout our lengthy partnership he made it a point to mention that, for honour's sake, I should register his mistakes along with his successes. And while I was reticent to do that, fearing a reduction in the high esteem with which the public held him; in this instance it was all but certain only he would ever know.

As the taxi took me down the long driveway to the main house, I could see the remains of Holmes' once-thriving apiary. A few wooden hives, long bereft of bees, were all that was left of his post-detecting occupation. I was let out near the door and paid the driver. As he pulled away I turned and stared for a moment at the front door; at a threshold which I had not crossed for some time. I might have stayed in my stationary position for an hour longer if I didn't hear a very familiar voice carry through an open window.

"It's open, Watson."

Without response I stepped forward and entered the dwelling; not sure in which condition I might find him. I walked through the front hallway and into his ground-floor living room, where I was surprised at the sight before me. If not for his affliction it might have been the 1880's in Baker Street once again. Holmes stood near the unlit fireplace; pipe in hand, a fragile, gaunt figure leaning against its mantle for support.

My instincts as a doctor involuntarily kicked in and, without applying much thought, I chastised him. "Really Holmes; smoking during the end stages of cancer?"

He smiled. "The operative words in your rebuke are "end stages," Watson. The fact is I would have been better served to have taken more seriously your reprimands on this filthy habit years ago. Now though as a man of medicine I must ask you: really, what difference does it make?"

Of course he was right. "Not much, I'm afraid."

"To deny myself even the simplest pleasures at this stage would be utterly pointless."

"Quite so," I agreed.

'Now then Watson, please. Have a seat." No sooner had he gestured toward an overstuffed chair did he break out in an ugly cough.

"Goodness, Holmes. Let me call for your nurse."

"I'm all right, my friend. Besides I've dismissed her from her duties for the next week."

"Dismissed her? What on Earth for?"

"It was not an easy task, Watson," he stated as if he hadn't heard my question. "As I have been in decline for some time, she has been with me for quite awhile. And I am rather certain I'll not see her again in this world." Holmes continued. "What for, you ask? My answer is two-fold. There is no need for her to see the sight which will shortly come to pass, and surely you'll be staying with me to the last. Who better should I hope to have by my side than the talented Dr. John H. Watson?"

Now it was my turn to smile. "A "talented" doctor who has long-since retired but, yes; of course I will be staying on with you as long as need be."

"Excellent. Before dispatching my nurse with your telegram I asked her to prepare an upstairs bedroom for you. I trust you will find your accommodations satisfactory, Watson. If not, take comfort in that you will not need to endure them very long."

"Come now, Holmes. A simple cot would be satisfactory. My only concern here is for your welfare."

"I'm afraid we are past that, my good fellow. Now, pray unpack your things and re-join me here for some brandy and reminiscing."

"Certainly. Ah, Holmes-" he cut me off.

"Second door on your right, Watson. Do take your time."

*   *   *

A short time later I returned downstairs dressed in a more comfortable fashion. Holmes was at his desk scratching on a sheet of paper. It amazed me how, at age seventy-six, he could still appear so much younger than his years. The cancer did little to diminish his genetic gifts.

"Am I interrupting, Holmes?"

"Not at all; I'll be done in a moment. I'm just adding to my will. I'd like to leave something to my nurse Christine for her extraordinary care during my difficulty. As an American who will in all probability send this unexpected bonus back home, I should like to provide her with an inheritance in dollars. She has been in my employ two-hundred eighty-three days, at five dollars per day ... " he began to calculate on a nearby piece of scrap paper.

"$1,415 dollars," said I absent-mindedly. Holmes threw me a cursory glance; then returned to his paper. Seconds later, he looked back up at me with a grin.

"So it is. Is it possible such an arithmetical proficiency has escaped my notice all these long years, Watson?"

I offered a small grunt. "Not in the slightest, Holmes. I've always had a thing for it."

"Yes, of course. At any rate I apologize for my brief segue into morbidity. However one or two unfortunate chores still remain." He let loose another coughing spasm, in the midst of which he removed a handkerchief from his pocket to place before his mouth.

"Holmes please let me get you something. I can prepare an elixir that should aid your burden."

He held up a hand to stop me. "Watson, these are trivial matters. I did not summon you here to be my manservant. As I've said, let's just talk; reminisce. That would be the most effective elixir of all, my friend." Holmes signed the document, replaced the pen in its holder, and walked gingerly to the couch.

His courage was extraordinary.

"As you wish, Holmes." I took a seat in an overstuffed chair facing him.

"Well now, my friend. Let's hear how you've been."

I offered up a smile. "Why don't you tell me, for

old time's sake?"

He didn't hesitate for even a moment. "All right, then. Your desire to socialize has significantly decreased, despite being retired with an abundance of free time with which to do so. You've finally taken to burying yourself in the classic literature you'd always meant to, but never made time for. Too, you've given up the rich desserts for which you've had a lifelong affinity. That is, of course, whenever I wasn't cutting dinner short to drag you into whatever crime-thwarting shenanigans were necessary at a given time. Lastly, in addition to providing me comfort, you've come here with something to tell me, and you're still debating the merits of doing so."

I was years past being surprised at Holmes's uncanny accuracy with his deductions, but that still did not reduce the level of my appreciation for his skill. As usual though, I had to know how he knew. "Excellent, Holmes. Need I even ask?"

He gave a gentle laugh. "No, I suppose not. Once more then for, as you call it, "old time's sake." When you arrived there was a button missing on your coat; a pet-peeve of yours which has always been addressed posthaste. The possibility does exist of it being lost en route here, of course. However if one were to combine it with the two-day's growth of stubble on your chin, along with the condition of your walking stick, then my deduction is all but confirmed."

"Stubble on my . . . " I started to say.

"Watson you received my telegraph this afternoon, did you not? If a gentleman has not shaven by the noon hours, he does not anticipate seeing anyone that day.

Too, your walking stick was coated up its bottom six inches with streaks of dried mud. The weather over the past week both here and in London has been dry and sunny; indicating not only has the mud been there for some time now, but also that its presence is of little importance to you. Along with your misplaced button, it adds up to you having not socialized in quite awhile. Since your time is your own, that can only mean that such a decision is voluntary."

"Ah, Holmes; this never gets old."

He continued on with his customary aplomb. "The angles of the prominent paper cuts located on the interior of both index fingers indicate that you have been reading for long stretches of time. In truth long enough so that the occasional switch of positions would bring much greater comfort. Thus, you would be required to turn pages with either hand as necessary. Since carelessness has never been your hallmark, the cuts can only indicate you have spent an inordinate amount of time reading. As it's unlikely you're re-reading your old medical textbooks, and newspapers would not take nearly the effort needed for you to flip pages to such an extent, what else is left but that dusty collection of un-read literary classics inhabiting your study?"

"And the desserts?"

"Elementary. The loose fit of your clothes and the addition of suspenders to your wardrobe signify an obvious loss of weight. Since you've been reclusive and have therefore partaken little in the way of exercise, the answer lies within your diet. That being the case, it is far more plausible that you would pass on the desserts rather than the actual meals. There you have it, Watson."

"Bravo, Holmes."

"My pleasure. It's good to know I'll go out with a success."

As the truth of his statement set in I felt the weight of his words. I then proceeded to ask him about the latter. "There is still the . . . "

" . . . matter of your untold tale?" He finished for me.

"Yes."

"Watson for that you must give credit more to my intuition than any deductive reasoning. I've known you for near six decades now, and I can tell when a thing vexes you. In this instance of course I had to assign a portion of your somewhat uncharacteristically hesitant demeanor since your arrival to concern for my unfortunate situation. That aside, there is indeed something more."

"Well then Holmes rest assured that your powers of intuition are equal to those of your observation. However, all in good time."

"As you wish Watson; although I'll point out that time is no longer a luxury for me."

"How much would you say?"

"Four days. No longer. In fact were you still a betting man and such things were wagered on in decent society, I'd advise you to place your money on 7 July, 1930."

"Holmes! How can you be so nonchalant about such a thing?"

"Watson, if there is one thing about me to be true

amongst all others, it would be that I am a man whose thoughts and actions are dictated almost entirely by logic. To function differently now, at the end, would be highly inconsistent. I believe the corresponding idiom is that a leopard does not change his spots."

"While that is true, it seems that in this situation there should be at least some thought given to the one mystery no man can solve."

"The answer to that mystery will come soon enough, Watson. And if death turns out to be nothing more than a dark oblivion, I should rather not waste my remaining ninety-six hours contemplating what I'll shortly know for certain."

"How can you know such a thing with that much precision?" I enquired.

"I'll grant that my exact hours remaining are an estimate. However I'm not ignorant of medical science, and I've done my research on both the subject and stages of cancer. And though I don't wish to spend the time it would take for a full conversation on the matter, I am confident in my diagnosis."

"I see. Well, it's your . . . "

" . . . funeral?"

"Stop that . . . " I bellowed. "I was going to say that that is your prerogative. I can't believe how light you're taking this situation."

"What shall I do then, eh? Mope my way along into the next world? The end is inevitable for us all; no one escapes. The only difference is the manner of the thing, and I'll add that few know that better than you, Doctor. Now, how about you help me make us dinner? I'm famished."

I could see there was no sense in trying to change his attitude. And really, why bother? That he should be in good spirits at such a time could only be a good thing, both medically and spiritually. I decided to drop it. "Yes. After having no lunch before the ride here I believe I could eat a horse."

*   *   *

We'd had a fine meal which we prepared together; something we'd never done even once during our long partnership in Baker Street due to the exquisite culinary skills of Mrs. Hudson. Afterward I built an unnecessary fire and we talked well into the night. I can attest that I did not retire until well past three o'clock. The next morning, 4 July, was another beautiful day, and Holmes lamented that he hadn't the strength for a walk around the grounds of his farm. Instead I helped him outside to a comfortable bench which he had installed some time ago just for days like this very one. To give him room I brought a separate chair out from the inside for me to rest on. For awhile we simply sat and watched the world in this serene setting. A stream babbled near one side of the property and the occasional bird landed nearby. It was as I was watching the latest one descend that Holmes finally spoke.

"You know, Watson, across the Atlantic today our American friends are celebrating their freedom. In a way I find that somewhat fitting. As I reflect back, my entire career has been about freedom; either working to avenge both those who had it prematurely stolen, or to justly assist in taking it away from those who did the stealing."

It had been quite some time since I had heard such a profound statement from him that was not in conjunction with an active case. I had also an inkling that he was not yet finished with his thought, so I said nothing. I was correct. He continued.

"The condition in which I now find myself could also be considered a freedom; freedom from this malady, and the tedium of life bereft of action. I must say that I am not afraid to face whatever comes next. In fact I look forward to a new set of challenges and puzzles to solve, presumably without the shackles of this affliction. And should there be nothing at all, I may lay down knowing I had a good run of it. Better than most, I daresay. Watson I believe we have made the world a better place for our fellow man, and there's not much more that can be asked of anyone."

"Quite so, quite so. Though I must say I hadn't thought about it in such a manner, Holmes."

"That is understandable, my friend. It is my belief that the man facing his own mortality is the man whose thoughts run deepest. What say you, Watson?"

"I haven't given it as much thought as you have, Holmes. Though at my advanced age, in truth I cannot say that contemplation of my own mortality hasn't been more frequent of late."

"Indeed. And is there anything born of that contemplation that you wish to discuss at this late date, Watson?" He prodded.

"Not tonight, my good man. For now I'd just like to enjoy this beautiful sunset with my oldest and dearest of friends."

"As you wish."

At that point silence won the day and we sat there, both marveling at the beauty of a sunset we had taken for granted all these many years.

*   *   *

That evening Holmes slept soundly, while I myself got nary a wink.

*   *   *

The next day, 5 July, went much like the previous. With the exception that Holmes's cough had increased noticeably since my arrival, necessitating we remain inside for the day. Later that evening, as on each one previous, I built a fire. As the sun went down once again I poured us each a brandy and handed Holmes his as he sat on the couch. I then retreated to my chair. After a moment or two, this time it was I who broke the silence.

"Holmes, you've had a career for the ages. Tell me, are you contented?"

"Ah, we've come to the mystery at last. I ask you, Watson. In going through your notes of late, have you come across a case that you believe wasn't adequately solved?"

I paused for a moment. "You might say that."

"And what else might I say?"

And so it was upon; the moment I'd not looked forward to in the least.

"In all of our years together my dear Holmes, it has been you who have crafted story after story for me through your fantastic intellect and the braveness of your actions. Tonight, I shall relate to you a story of my own. Due to its nature, which you will soon enough learn, you'll forgive me in advance if I do this in my own way; in my own time."

"I can assure you that you have my undivided attention, Watson. Pray continue." In the background the fireplace crackled sporadically.

"Yes, well. I'll start in the years prior to when our mutual friend Stamford introduced us. I've never told you much about that time." I paused briefly. Holmes looked upon me transfixed. On my honour, though I had not yet divulged a single thing of consequence, I believe he had already known that this was to be a tale of great significance. He remained silent. I continued. "Growing up I had wanted more out of life than what I recognized fate had likely prescribed for me. I had little desire for money; aside from procuring enough to live in relative comfort. What I wanted was respect; to leave my mark on the world in some lasting way beyond that of whatever I might accomplish through a traditional vocation. Whatever my future had in store for me I wanted to create something, to be a leader of men. Later, of course, to get myself started in the world I became a doctor and a surgeon."

"And a fine one at that," he interjected.

"Thank you, my friend. A compliment from you is high praise indeed." I paused there for a moment, wondering if I should go on. While Holmes's eyes were as bright as ever, the rest of him was clearly wasting away. Why continue? I thought. Then I realized the irrevocable decision was made the moment I'd opened my mouth. I pressed on.

"As you know, after medical school I went into the army and saw action on multiple fronts. Being so close to death on a daily basis cemented in me how brief life can be for any of us. I decided to try and form a local society, with me at its head. To get started, during my turn in the Second Anglo-Afghan War I began by building my foundation with two loyal individuals. First I recruited a former theatre student who'd been drafted; Jacob McCutcheon by name. Next, there was a relatively obscure Colonel who, though older than I and rank notwithstanding, was more of a follower than a leader. His taste for violence was in excess of any soldier I had known. He seemed almost disappointed when his tour ended." I paused a moment. "Before I go on Holmes, I have to say how difficult it is for me to reveal this less honourable side of my personality to you, cultivated during my youth, in fear that it may diminish whatever standing I may have gained in your eyes."

He began to speak, then broke out into his most violent coughing spasm yet. When it subsided, he spoke rather coldly. "Watson this has the feel of a church confessional and, like any priest worth his salt, I cannot make a sound judgment until I hear the entire list of transgressions. Please continue."

Though his words were not very comforting; comfort is not really what I deserved. "As I've said, I had no personal desire for wealth. However it was to an extent necessary if I was to draw in more recruits to the small, clandestine organization I was beginning to form. In the time before our meeting, Holmes, I was a man of more questionably morality." Holmes's brow creased as if he had now started in earnest the motor on his intellect, and was half lost in thought because of it. Still, he remained silent.

"The assemblage that had begun to take shape was initially intended to be along the same secretive, peaceful lines of the Freemasons, nothing more; only with our own rites and rituals. However that was not to be. What the three of us ended up attracting was a sort of, well, moderately intelligent riff-raff short on morals who didn't seem to have a place in decent society. Things then began to expand much more rapidly than I had foreseen. The peaceful society I had envisioned had begun turning into one made up of criminals, with criminal intent. And while I had wanted the admiration of others for myself, I knew I could never be respected as the head of such a group of scoundrels. But it had already been set too far in motion. I then took McCutcheon and the Colonel into my confidence and, for our benefit, constructed a back-story based on another particular talent of mine, as well as a plan that I had come up with. The primary goal of which was to build up for my alias a reputation of intolerance for disloyalty. It was to be spread about that I possessed a great intellect, and had no issues applying brute force when necessary to keep our members in line. The stronger the reputation, the more apt it was that a fear of potential repercussions for disobedience would itself do the trick. Unfortunately, at times it required more than just fear. That was where the Colonel came in." I paused to take a sip of my brandy. Holmes had closed his eyes but, as I well knew, was anything but asleep.

"At any rate, since those two had done the initial subsequent recruiting, and then had the new members enlist more members on their own; my own true identity was unknown to none but them. As part of the plan I made them both de facto heads of my organization. McCutcheon was the face and the Colonel, the muscle. As I've mentioned, I possessed a proficiency in more than just surgery, and I taught McCutcheon of it what I could. Expertly forged documents, including a degree from a small university, provided legitimacy to his claims that he was highly regarded in his false profession. Also, I was always there to assist either by telegram or, when need be, in person. Outwardly, I continued my practice as a doctor and some time later is when Stamford introduced us. Though at that time I hadn't yet heard of you, it didn't take me long as your flat mate to recognize the sheer magnitude of your intellect. It clearly rivaled and, in fact, exceeded my own. I realized how fortunate I was not only to be privy to your methods and genius, but also to be able to keep firsthand tabs on your progress tracking the criminal element in London. Including that contained within the organization which I myself had inadvertently built and kept in regular contact with."

Holmes opened his emotionless eyes and looked directly at me. "I have met this McCutcheon, have I not?"

"Yes, on two occasions."

"Indeed. And unless I'm very much mistaken he was a far greater actor than you have given him credit for." I nodded in agreement. "Just to substantiate my suspicions Watson, where is Jacob McCutcheon at present?"

I paused a moment before answering. "In Switzerland, currently residing at the bottom of the Reichenbach Falls." The silence between us was deafening, and spoke volumes. It lasted nearly a minute before Holmes broke it. "And the full name of your other accomplice?"

Once again I hesitated briefly; then continued. "Colonel Sebastian Moran." This was met with more silence, until this time I spoke up. "Sherlock Holmes, allow me to formally introduce myself. I am Dr. John H. Watson, M.D. Known also in some circles as Professor James Moriarity."

It was clear to me that Holmes had already solved this puzzle at some point during my story, but he either didn't want to believe it or was just waiting for a confirmation. I had given him one; both now and for all time.

"Watson, you have successfully perpetrated the largest deception on me that I could ever possibly conceive. And that is no small task."

"If it means anything Holmes, my affection and admiration for you is, and always has been, completely and wholeheartedly genuine."

"A very small consolation, Watson."

"Perhaps, but it's important to know that the seeds of my organization were sewn before we'd met, and there was no plausible way to disband it by that point. As your reputation as a consulting detective grew in London, I told McCutcheon and Moran that my continued stay as your flat mate was due to it being the perfect cover. Such a thing was easy for them to accept because it made such perfect sense. They remained loyal to me till the very end."

"Pity I cannot say the same of you, Watson. You tried to have me killed!"

"You must understand that by the time of the Reichenbach my loyalties had long since transferred over to you, but there was nothing I could do. My choices were to give myself up or trust in your abilities to get yourself out of that situation; which of course you did." He scoffed at me; I let it pass. "Shall I fill you in on the details, Holmes?"

"No need. Just tell me if I have it correct, Watson. You maintained the position as absentee leader of your crime syndicate for years; as you've said, ceding almost completely the reins of the day-to-day operations to McCutcheon and Moran. They became quite proficient at running things; and at a huge profit for themselves thanks to your generosity. It's no wonder they had developed such loyalty to you. You gave them what they never would have gained otherwise; their own positions of leadership, respect-as misplaced as it may be-and significant wealth. This went on for years until, unbeknownst to me; you discovered that I had finally picked up the scent of your syndicate's trail. At this point I'd like to pause and commend you on your own acting skills, Watson. You never let on a thing and, until this very trip to Sussex, had not once let slip any elevated proficiency with mathematics whatsoever. Maybe here you did so subconsciously, so that I might deduce this myself and therefore spare you the trouble and pain of relating it. Maybe you didn't. Either way your performance over the years has been so convincing that I paid even the slightest connection between you and Moriarity no mind whatsoever." Though still calm, his voice was tinged with anger.

"Holmes, our friendship was not an act, it-" he cut me off.

"I'm not finished, Watson. Please grant me the courtesy of doing so." I nodded. He continued. "While pretending to be oblivious to the whole matter, you had discovered that I was casting a wide net out for Moriarity. Further, you were fully aware that I had not known either what he looked like or that his name was, in actuality, an alias. In response, you went to McCutcheon, familiarized him with me and my methods, and sent him to Baker Street in the guise of the great mathematics "Professor." This also clears up yet another mystery, Watson. I had often wondered why a ruthless criminal mastermind would show up at my door, unarmed, and bearing a warning which included the opportunity to go about my business should I only back down from pursuing him. I can't imagine such a courtesy was ever extended to other, less formidable opponents of yours, Watson."

"No." I answered flatly. "It was not prudent if we were to maintain the illusion that we were an organization to be feared."

"I suppose it never occurred to you that, by following through with actual violence, you were assuring that a fear of your organization was no "illusion" at all.

"It had all gotten out of hand, Holmes."

"That is certainly an understatement. When I did not relent, you set up the meeting with McCutcheon-as-Moriarity at Reichenbach. At the top you had your own currier send you a note which you'd drafted yourself, allowing you to conveniently exit the scene. Undoubtedly you took that time to instruct a heretofore hidden Moran where to position himself in the event that I emerged the victor."

"As I've told you, with very little choice in the matter I had to trust in you to get yourself out of it, Holmes. Moran knew about the plan; having been present when I created it with McCutcheon. I had to give him a part; not to would have been too suspicious. And if I hadn't, he would've shown up anyway."

"You may justify it all you wish, Watson. The fact is you wagered my own life. You, the very same man to whom I'd entrusted it so many times before."

"Holmes . . . " He waved me off.

"This can only mean you knew for the entirety of my three year self-imposed absence that I had survived at Reichenbach; as Moran certainly would have reported as much to you"

"Yes."

"This also explains his reticence to speak when we caught him in the act with his air rifle in the empty house upon my "resurrection." That must have been tremendously awkward for you both, Watson; with him not expecting to see you. Perhaps you didn't have time to notify him of my plan; or perhaps you were hoping that I would fatally injure him during his apprehension and free you from your torturous predicament once and for all. Whatever the truth, Moran clearly believed it to be the former as you both managed to play it off as if you were perfect strangers. That is loyalty indeed, Watson. Another magnificent performance; kudos to you both. The pull you had over your minions was certainly extraordinary." I bowed my head, as there was no reasonable retort.

"With McCutcheon resting at the depths of the Reichenbach and Moran off to the gallows, there was no one left to identify you. Since I had conveniently rounded up the rest of "Moriarity's" gang for Lestrade, you were fully in the clear. At that point you simply remained silent until this very day. Was your wife in on this, I wonder?"

"Of course not, Holmes. Whatever you may now think of me, she was nothing short of an angel."

"In other words, she was a good woman who was also deceived." For this too, there was no answer.

"So what now?" I asked sullenly.

"What now?' He responded, with an air of genuine surprise. "There is no "what now," Watson. You have won. I am immobile, there is no telephone here, and I shall be forever gone within two days."

"I didn't win anything, Holmes. If you only could know how much I wish I'd never started any of this so long ago."

"Don't waste your breath on me, Watson. If there is a Maker, you may explain it to Him. It may be a day, a week, or a decade, but your time will come soon enough."

"Please, I don't wish to see things end this way. I am exceedingly repentant. I speak in earnest."

"Speak however you'd like. The fact remains that I have devoted my life to catching every kind of criminal, and stopping every kind of villainy in its very tracks. I have brought justice to everyone from kings to the lowliest peasants. And now, in the last hours of my life, I discover that through it all, the man I thought my best-my only-friend, my most trusted confident, was in truth my most detested adversary." He then abruptly turned away, and uttered not a single word more to me that evening.

*   *   *

He had not spoken at all the next day either, as his condition had worsened dramatically in the night. He was confined to the couch and prone to nearly continuous coughing spasms. I watched over him; bringing him water and fresh blankets regularly. I was worried he wouldn't last the day; but once again he prevailed over his sickness. In the afternoon I had built what was to be my last fire in Sussex, and adjusted his couch toward it. It was an easy task, as my friend seemed to weigh no more than eight stone.

Though I had more than earned his silence, I did not wish our last hours to pass with such animosity between us. Then, shortly after midnight, he took another turn for the worse. I pulled up my chair, gave him more water, and intermittently wiped his brow. This went on for some time. In fact, I'd lost complete track of it whilst we remained quietly by the fireplace. The silence was broken at last by the playing of Westminster Quarters on the mantle clock, followed by four chimes. I glanced outside through the window and saw that the full darkness of night still held the land firmly within its grasp. It was a raspy voice calling for my attention that brought me back to reality. I looked down at Holmes, who was trying to speak. I lowered myself nearer to him so as to not miss what he wished to say. The crackling of the fire was the only other sound to be heard.

"Watson . . . "

"Yes, Holmes. I'm here." With no small effort he reached out with his right hand and took in it my left.

"My time is nearly done. I shall not hear that clock strike five; of this I am certain. Listen to me now, Watson. What you've revealed to me is dreadful. However it is not for me to judge you. It is clear that you are indeed earnest about your desire to repent and that may count for something. How much, if anything, I know not. What I know to be true is that you are sincere in your words regarding the importance of our acquaintance. Also, you had no small part in helping me to bring countless villains into the Yard. That, too, may work in your favor if and when your Judgment Day arrives. For me the paradox lies in that, though you were London's greatest criminal mind, you were also my greatest friend. Possibly I should credit the former for pushing me into striving to leave my mark as the utmost champion of justice there has yet been. Or perhaps it's merely an irrational attempt to justify my remaining affection for you, Watson." He let go of my hand and readjusted himself into a position of greater comfort.

"Holmes, I . . . " For one last time, he cut me off.

"No," he looked up at me. "It's not necessary." He paused, and then uttered his last words in this world. "We are who we are, Watson. Preordained or not, for the better or the worse; each with our own parts to play. Now old friend, it has come time for me to surrender myself to eternity. Perhaps we shall meet again in a place where a greater understanding of such things is possible. Good-bye, Watson." With that he closed his eyes. He laid there for some time; his breathing laboured. Then, suddenly, it stopped altogether. I looked up at the clock through eyes welling with tears and saw that it was 4:51a.m., Monday 7 July, 1930. He had called it exactly; his powers remaining with him until the very end.

*   *   *

For six months after the death of Sherlock Holmes my conscience worked on me like never before. None of this was right; I deserved whatever I was to get. In thinking it over, I weighed the consequences of bringing the truth to light. How would such an action impact the renowned legacy of the world's greatest detective? Would his cases be reviewed anew with the thought that perhaps some impropriety had taken place, real or imagined, due to his long association with me? In truth he had never even the slightest idea of my duel identity; but that mattered little. Whoever on Earth would believe that the unequaled intellect of the great Sherlock Holmes could not detect London's foremost criminal mind living underneath his very roof, eating his very food, and sharing his every confidence? To the public such a thought would be ludicrous. So what was the point? Moran and McCutcheon were long since in their graves, and the rank and file scoundrels in my defunct organization had long ago been rounded up by Holmes himself and brought before their various magistrates. I myself was on the verge of entering my eighties and, as Holmes had correctly observed, would soon be answering to a much higher court than any to be found in the whole of the United Kingdom.

Ultimately I decided to leave my incarnate fate up to chance and speak directly with the one person who on a professional level knew Holmes and me better than anyone; the only man who could fairly assess the situation. And also judge as to whether the irreversible impact such a revelation would do to Holmes's legacy, and to no small extent the public perception of the London police force, was worth stringing up a tired old man. Then I would do whatever he advised.

*   *   *

Once I had determined over the Christmas holiday that this was the course I was going to take, I could think of no more fitting a time than Holmes's birthday to visit the man I was going to speak with. And so I had waited for this specific date. Now, it was upon. 6 January 1931 was a bitterly cold Tuesday morning, and snow was in the air when I walked up the steps and into Scotland Yard.

I entered the lobby and approached the desk where a Captain and Leftenant were conversing. I knew the former and, upon noticing me, he raised a hand in greeting.

"Doctor Watson! How good to see you," he exclaimed while extending his hand.

"Likewise, Captain Talbot." I answered while shaking it.

He turned toward the other man and motioned him over. "Alec, come here please. Doctor, I'd like to introduce you to Leftenant Alec Dalton."

I shook his hand as well. "Leftenant. Good to meet you."

"And you, sir. You wouldn't by any chance be the Doctor Watson who . . . "

"He is one and the same," Talbot interrupted with a broad smile.

"Well," Dalton continued, "let me just say sir that this is truly an honour."

"You make much of nothing, Leftenant. Holmes was the genius." He was about to protest when I cut him off. "Gentlemen, I do not wish to interrupt your day. I just stopped in for a small piece of information."

"Why of course, Doctor," Talbot answered. Whatever I may do to assist.

"Thank you, Captain. I am much indebted. Certainly by now Inspector Lestrade is retired; so I was wondering if I might have his current address in order to call on him. I have a message of some importance." The instantaneous frowns into which both faces in front of me simultaneously melted told me that the news I was about to hear would not be good.

Talbot glanced briefly at Dalton and then looked back toward me. "Unfortunately your timing could not be worse, Doctor. We received word this very morning that the Inspector had passed away only yesterday."

"Oh, no," said I. "How dreadful. We worked together for many years on many a case. He was a good man. Please accept my most heartfelt condolences, gentlemen." Both men thanked me. Then Talbot spoke.

"Is there something that we might assist you with, Doctor Watson?" I thought on it for a moment, and then made my decision. "No. Thank you though. The message to Lestrade was more along the lines of a personal nature."

"I see."

"Well Gentlemen, I've taken up more than enough of your morning already. Captain Talbot, Leftenant Dalton; I thank you for your time."

"Of course, Doctor. You're always welcome here," Talbot responded.

I smiled at them both, turned, and walked out of Scotland Yard. It would be the last time I'd ever see its inside.

Epilogue

That I had specifically waited until Holmes's birthday to talk with Lestrade, only to discover he had passed away the day before, seemed like some kind of sign to me. I do not put much stock in such claptrap as the supernatural; but I also don't put much stock in coincidence, either. Holmes himself taught me that. If there was some method for my friend to signal me on which way to proceed, out of anyone I'd ever known, I'm certain he'd be the one to find it.

Regardless, I had a difficult time reconciling that my legacy would remain unscathed after what I had done. After much internal debate, these tapes became a compromise. To reiterate what I have stated prior to beginning this tale, once I'm gone I shall have no more say in the matter, so I'll leave them behind to the whim of fate. If their destiny is to be swallowed up by some mechanical shovel years hence should my home ever be razed, then so be it. Alternatively, if their destiny is to be discovered and published, then so be it, too. I have of late considered that nothing, not even my final revelation, would do much to damage the reputation of such a great man as Sherlock Holmes. He will rightly live forever in high esteem within the hearts and minds of not only his admiring countrymen, but the entire world inclusive.

Fittingly I dictate these words on the tenth anniversary of Holmes's death which is, ironically, my own birthday. And once I lay down this microphone I shall never utter another remark for publication.

With the story now told, I shall leave you with this. Whatever judgment is placed upon me by posterity, I should like it to be known that Sherlock Holmes redeemed me in every way. He gave my life far more purpose than I had earned or deserved; and taught me the value of virtue and morality. For that I shall be forever grateful. If only I had met him earlier, I am certain I would have learned these lessons in time to avoid making the poor choices of my younger days. Whether I shall pay for my past transgressions in the next world remains yet to be seen. In any event, I am ready.

Dr. John H. Watson, M.D.

7 July 1940

Acknowledgment

No literary work recounting the characters of Sherlock Holmes and Dr. Watson can be written without a show of gratitude for their originator, Sir Arthur Conan Doyle. Doyle's creations are timeless, beloved, and have always been among my favorites. Along with Charles Dickens' *A Christmas Carol*, they were this American's introduction into the remarkable world of British literature. While it was a difficult decision to portray Dr. Watson in the manner in which he is shown in this work, after coming up with the idea, I was enthralled with the prospect of presenting a completely fresh take on the Holmes' stories. Nothing more. The reality is, to me Watson in his greatest incarnations will always be depicted as the upstanding, moralistic and ever-caring best friend to Holmes that he always was.

–Chris Gay
  Hartford, Connecticut USA

About the Author

Chris Gay is an author, freelance writer, voice-over artist, broadcaster and actor. He writes and broadcasts a daily, minute radio humor spot in Hartford, Connecticut. He's also written the paranormal, theological thriller novel *Ghost of a Chance* and three humor books: *And That's the Way It Was...Give or Take: A Daily Dose of My Radio Writings, Shouldn't Ice Cold Beer Be Frozen? My 365 Random Thoughts to Improve Your Life Not One Iota,* and *The Bachelor Cookbook: Edible Meals with a Side of Sarcasm.* He's been published nationally in Writer's Digest and is currently writing his fourth and fifth humor books, *Another Round of Ice Cold Beer: My 365 More Random Thoughts to Improve Your Life Not One Iota* and *Something Witty this Way Comes;* the latter being a collection of pieces written for his humor blog. Also, he's writing the *Ghost of a Chance* sequel *Perdition's Wrath,* and has written and voiced radio commercials, authored both comedic and non-comedic freelance articles, scripts, press releases, website, media and technical content, done occasional radio color commentary for local sports, and acted in a couple of movies and plays. His website is chrisjgay.com, and his humor blog can be found at chrisgay.wordpress.com. He lives in Connecticut.

The Time Has Come

Sherlock Holmes and the Final Reveal

As the end draws near for long-retired Sherlock Holmes in Sussex Downs, he calls one last time for the company of his best friend and colleague, Dr. John Watson. What was meant to be four last days of camaraderie and reminiscing instead leads to the most shocking, explosive revelation both of the great detective's career, and his life.

Sherlock Holmes and the Final Reveal is a Holmes tale like none other ever conceived. Fans of Baker Street's legendary detective will be left with the insatiable need to contemplate its extraordinary conclusion forevermore.

www.chrisjgay.com

"When a doctor does go wrong he is the first of criminals. He has nerve and he has knowledge."

–Sir Arthur Conan Doyle

www.ingramcontent.com/pod-product-compliance
Lightning Source LLC
Chambersburg PA
CBHW061457170626
46811CB00004B/1559